What's up, Jac?
Rob Lewis

PONT

Jac had a farm on a hilltop in Wales
With views of the river and mountains and vales.
Being up so high meant Jac's callers were rare
But Jac wasn't lonely with his animals there.

What's up, Jac?

First Impression – 2004

ISBN 1 84323 428 9

© illustrations and text: Rob Lewis

This title is published with the financial support of the
Welsh Books Council.

Cover design: Olwen Fowler

Printed in Wales at
Gomer Press, Llandysul, Ceredigion

They all lived together content on the land
Until an old man came with poster in hand.

'The farm in the valley is having a sale,'
He said, as Ceridwen the cow swished her tail.
'There's tractors and bailers and tethers and rings.'
'Yes,' said Jac, smiling. 'I could do with those things.'

He pinned up the poster so he wouldn't forget
Next to the number for Megan the vet.
The animals peered through the window to see.
They stayed there all evening while Jac had his tea.
'There's something quite strange in the way that they gaze,'
He said, feeling puzzled. 'They're all in a daze.'

Ceridwen the cow he put back in her shed

While Gwenda the sheepdog lay down in her bed.

Heulwen the hen Jac returned to her nest
And Catrin the cat came inside for a rest.

Pegi the pig he led back to her sty

And Siani the sheep to a field nearby.

But Ceridwen the cow mooed and mooed through the night,
While Gwenda howled loudly and gave Jac a fright.

Next morning Siani seemed in a sad mood
And Pegi the pig had gone off her food.

Heulwen the hen in her coop had stopped laying
And even poor Catrin the cat wasn't playing.

Nothing had changed after two weeks or more
So Jac thought of calling the vet for a cure.
Jac phoned up Megan who came right away.
She shook her head slowly and said with dismay,
'For twenty-five years I've been a farm vet
And this is the strangest case I've found yet.
P'raps it's the weather or even the food.
Maybe they're just in an odd sort of mood.
It could be depression or animal 'flu –
But to be honest, I haven't a clue.'

Megan went home leaving Jac without hope.

If things got worse how on earth could he cope?

He went to bed early with a bowl of hot cawl

To the sound of moo-mooing and Gwenda's loud howl.

But when he woke up he could not hear a sound

So he got out of bed and had a look round.

Gwenda and Catrin were not in the house.
Even the farmyard was quiet as a mouse.
Ceridwen the cow had gone from her stall
And Heulwen the hen he could not find at all.

For Siani and Pegi he searched every place
But of sheep or of pig there wasn't a trace.

Jac stared at the ground wondering what he should do
When suddenly there in the mud was a clue.
Footprints led down to the valley below.
That's odd, thought Jac. Let's see where they go.

He followed them down to a farm in the vale.

This was the place that was having the sale.

As he opened the gate he saw a strange sight.

All of his animals cuddled up tight

With partners they'd found right there on the farm.

'What's going on here, then?' Jac said in alarm.

Then he realised, 'Good heavens above,
All of my animals have fallen in love!'
Jac remembered the poster at home
And thought of the reason they wanted to roam –
The poster displayed the most handsome males
That had ever been seen in that part of Wales.
It had caused each creature to daydream and start
To search for the one that had captured her heart.

So Siani found Gareth, a ram with fine wool
And Ceridwen the cow met Caradoc the bull.

Then Heulwen the hen found a cockerel named Dyl
And Catrin met Tomos and Pegi met Bil.

And finally Gwenda who was feeling quite shy
Was licked on the nose by a sheepdog called Dai.

Jac's animals couldn't stay there, he was sure,
So he went to the farmhouse and knocked at the door.

But when the door opened he started to stutter.
His legs were like jelly and his heart was a-flutter
'Hello,' said the girl. 'My name's Tracey Bevan.'
'H-hello,' said Jac shyly, 'I think I'm in heaven!'

Jac drove straight to town and bought her a ring.
Then they got married the following Spring.

So Tracey and Jac put their two farms together.
And now they'll live happily for ever and ever.